An I Can Read Book®

Emma's MAGIC WINTER

story by Jean Little
pictures by Jennifer Plecas

HarperCollins*Publishers*

HarperCollins®, ▭®, and I Can Read Book®
are trademarks of HarperCollins Publishers Inc.

Emma's Magic Winter
Text copyright © 1998 by Jean Little
Illustrations copyright © 1998 by Jennifer Plecas
Printed in the U.S.A. All rights reserved.

Library of Congress Cataloging-in-Publication Data
Little, Jean, 1932–
    Emma's magic winter / story by Jean Little ; pictures by Jennifer Plecas.
      p.   cm. —(An I can read book)
    Summary: With the help of her new friend who has magic boots just like her
own, Emma overcomes her shyness and no longer hates reading out loud in
school.
    ISBN 0-06-025389-4. — ISBN 0-06-025390-8 (lib. bdg.)
    [1. Bashfulness—Fiction. 2. Magic—Fiction. 3. Friendship—Fiction.
4. Schools—Fiction.] I. Plecas, Jennifer, ill. II. Title. III. Series.
PZ7.L7225Em 1998   97-49667
[E]—dc21   CIP
                                               AC

1 2 3 4 5 6 7 8 9 10

❖

First Edition

Visit us on the World Wide Web!
http://www.harperchildrens.com

for Bill Morris,
who urged me to try again
—J.L.

for Tomo
—J.P.

CONTENTS

New Neighbors

Emma liked reading to herself.

But she did not like

reading out loud.

"Your turn, Emma,"

said her teacher, Mr. Kent.

"Speak up, so we can hear."

Emma tried, but she was shy.

She could only whisper.

On Friday Mom picked Emma up
from school.

She said, "We have new neighbors.

The Grays have two children.

Josh is four and Sally is your age.

You can make friends."

"I don't know how," Emma said.

The next day Mom made pies.

"Get your boots, Emma," she said.

"Please take this pie to the Grays."

"Come with me, Mom,"

begged Emma.

"Be brave, Emma," Mom said.

"Sally is new and needs a friend."

"Go for it, Emma," Dad said.

"You can't be shy with a pie."

"But what do I say?"

asked Emma.

"Start with 'Hi,'"

Mom told her.

Emma Meets Sally

Emma took the pie to the Grays.

She knocked on the door and waited.

Sally opened the door.

"Hi," said Emma and Sally

at the same time.

"Mom sent you this pie," Emma said.

"Thanks," Sally said.

She took the pie to her mom.

16

While Emma waited by the door,

she saw Sally's snow boots.

They were the same as hers.

Then Sally came back.

Emma did not know what to say.

She looked down at her boots.

The boots gave her an idea.

She took a deep breath.

"Are your boots magic?"

"What?" said Sally.

Emma talked fast.

"My boots have magic powers.

They can make me vanish.

They can even make me fly.

Your boots look just like mine.

Are yours magic too?"

"I don't know," Sally said slowly.

"I never tried them out."

"Lunchtime," called Sally's mom.

"Let's try my boots out after lunch,"
Sally said.

"Come to my house," said Emma.

"Okay," said Sally.

"See you," Emma said, and smiled.

Making friends was easy.

Maybe her boots really were magic!

After Lunch

Emma waited for Sally outside.

"Magic Boots, make me vanish,"
Emma said.

"What did you say?" said Sally.

"I told my boots to make me vanish."

"When will they do it?" Sally asked.

"They did it already," said Emma.

"If you still see me,

your boots are magic too."

"I still see you," said Sally.

"Now make *me* vanish, Emma."

"You have to do it yourself,"

said Emma.

"Say, 'Magic Boots,

make me vanish.'"

Sally said it.

"Great!" said Emma.

"Now nobody sees you but me."

Sally grinned.

A woman and her baby came by.

"She can't see us," Emma said.

"Jump, Sally, jump!"

They jumped out of the way.

The baby waved to them.

"Babies know magic," said Emma.

Sally and Emma waved back.

Emma forgot she was shy.

Sally forgot she was new.

They were magic friends.

Josh

Sally's brother, Josh, came out.

"Where are you, Sally?" he called.

"Boots, let him see us," Emma said.

"Play with me, Sally," said Josh.

"This is my brother," Sally told Emma.

"His name is Josh, and he is a pest."

"I wish I had a little brother,"
Emma said.

"Don't tell your magic boots.

Don't do it, Emma," Sally said.

"Little brothers are big pests."

"Go away, yucky Sally," said Josh.

"I want Emma to make a fort
with me."

"Let Sally help," Emma said.

They all worked on the fort.

Then they went inside to play.

"Sally, I need your help

for a minute," said Mrs. Gray.

"Read to me, Emma," Josh said.

Emma did not want to read out loud.

But she liked Josh.

The book he held out was small.

Emma started to read to him.

It was easy.

Josh ran and got another book.

"Now read this one, Emma," he said.

When Sally came back,

Emma stopped.

It was time for her to go home.

"Did you make a friend?" Dad asked.

"Two friends," said Emma.

Mountain Climbers

The next day, Sally said,

"Mom says that I'll be in your class

at school."

"Great!" Emma said.

"But let's not talk about school.

Let's be mountain climbers."

"You find a rope," said Sally.

"I will find a mountain."

Emma ran for her dad's rope.

Sally found a big snowbank.

"Magic Boots, make this a mountain.

Make us mountain climbers,"

Sally said.

Sally pulled Emma up the mountain.

Then Emma pulled Sally up.

They slid down.

"Thank you, Emma," Sally said.

"You saved my life."

"You saved mine too," said Emma.

Sally and Emma played until dark.

"I am glad we are friends," Sally said.

"I won't feel shy at school tomorrow."

Emma went home slowly.

Tomorrow Sally would hear her read.

She would hear Mr. Kent say,

"Speak up, Emma."

"Boots, make school vanish," Emma said.

School

On Monday, Sally read first.

"Very good, Sally," Mr. Kent said.

"Now it is your turn, Emma."

Emma hung her head and whispered.

"Try to speak up, Emma,"

said Mr. Kent.

The recess bell rang.

"Emma can read after recess,"

Mr. Kent said.

Sally and Emma went outside.

"I wish I could read like you,"

Emma said.

"Emma, I heard you read to Josh.

You are a good reader," Sally said.

Emma looked down.

"Reading to Josh is easy," she said.

"Reading at school is not."

49

"Why not?" asked Sally.

"When they all look at me,

I try to speak up," said Emma.

"But only a whisper comes out."

Sally looked at Emma for a minute.

"I have an idea," she said.

"When we go in, keep your boots on.

Say, 'Magic Boots, make me brave.

Make me a good reader.'"

"It won't help," said Emma.

"It can't hurt to try," Sally said.

51

Emma kept her boots on.

Mr. Kent gave her the book.

Emma stood tall.

"Magic Boots, help," she whispered.

Then she began to read.

She read in a loud, clear voice.

"Good for you," said Mr. Kent.

"Way to go, Emma!" Sally said.

"Your magic boots did it."

"With the help of my magic friend,"

said Emma.

No Snow

All winter, the girls made magic.

They played with Josh, too,

and Emma read him lots of books.

But they liked their magic boots best.

When spring came, Mom said,

"It's time to put those boots away."

"But I need them," said Emma.

Mom held out a skipping rope.

"Try this instead," she said.

The rope was new with red handles.

Emma liked it a lot.

But what if Sally hated skipping?

"I want my boots," Emma said.

Dad looked out the window.

"Sally has her rope," he said.

Emma ran to look.

"Emma, let's skip," Sally called.

Sally's rope was new

with red handles,

just like Emma's.

Emma took the rope.

Dad opened the door for her.

Emma skipped out the door.

"Magic Rope, make me fly!"

she shouted.

"Great idea, Emma!" shouted Sally.

"Magic Rope, make me fly too."

Then Emma and Sally flew.

They flew into a magic spring.